To the children of the world—
may all your friends be truly sweet jelly beans.

MEAN, MEAN, NOT A Jelly Bean

By Mary Duchesne O'Donnell, RN, BSN
Illustrated by Rosanne O'Donnell

Jelly beans are wonderful,
sweet, and tart.
They make you feel good
deep, down in your heart.

Whether they're red, yellow,
purple, or green---
they're yum, yum, yummy!
Hurray jelly beans!

Friends come in all colors,
just like jelly beans.
And best of all, friends
try not to be mean.

Good friends are kind
and want to play fair.
They help when you're hurt,
and show you they care.

Good friends are a treat,
like sweet jelly beans.
They are never, ever
mean, mean, mean.

One day Lizzy wanted
to play at the park,
to skip, climb, run,
and jump until dark.

She went there to play
with all the girls and boys,
to have a happy time
and share in the joy.

But today a new boy, Sam,
played on the swings.
He was tall, cute, and seemed
to know everything.

Sam told the kids how
to play every game.
He told them what to do
and called them by name.

Lizzy was impressed
and ran to join the fun,
but then she noticed
how things were being done.

When his parents weren't looking
and no adults could see,
Sam pushed a smaller boy
right out of a tree.

When the little boy cried
after he fell,
Sam just laughed and said,
"You better not tell!"

He bossed around the kids
in an unkind way,
then pinched a girl, and laughed
when she screamed and ran away.

Then Sam's mother asked,
"O my precious son,
are you having fun and
being kind to everyone?"

He answered,
"Yes, Mommy, you know me.
I am always polite
and as kind as can be."

Lizzy could not believe it.
She felt so sad.
Sam -- was lying!
He was being so bad!

Then Sam turned to Lizzy

and said, "Go away!

Girls are not allowed

in this game that we play.

This park is for boys.

We're here to play ball.

Girls are too slow.

They don't play well at all."

He added, "Girls are weak

and stupid too."

Lizzy felt so bad,

she didn't know what to do.

Lizzy was so scared

and angry inside.

Should she tell a grown-up?

Should she run and hide?

This boy was the meanest

Lizzy had ever seen.

He was mean, mean, mean!

Not a jelly bean!

Then Lizzy stopped and listened

to that voice inside.

It said, *"Turn around, get away,*

and it's okay to cry."

Lizzy heard another voice
that made her smile.
It was Grace's!
They'd been friends for a while.

Grace called to Lizzy,
"Come play over here.
We're having such fun
and we want you near."

When Lizzy saw Grace with
Audrey, Celia, and Arlo,
she knew who to run to
and where she should go.

Soon all the kids ran
away from the boy
who was so mean
and destroying their joy.

The kids said, "Let's play games
that include everyone!
Games that are fair, gentle,
and lots of fun."

Sam stared at first,
but then walked away.
No one wanted to play with him
anymore that day.

Even kids who are tall,
cute, and smart
can be mean to others,
and hurt them in their hearts.

So here are some tips Lizzy has for you.
They are simple and easy to do.

If someone makes you cry
and they don't seem to care,
that is a strong warning
for you to beware!

If someone hits you
and then says, "You better not tell,"
that's another clue
that's clear as a bell.

If someone calls you names,
or tries to knock you down,
then you know for sure
you don't want them around.

These things are tricky!
Kids may try to defend
whatever they do
and still say they're your friend.

Lizzy learned an important
lesson that day.
She learned how to stay safe
when a mean kid wants to play.

Lizzy learned that she needs to
keep her good friends near
and listen to her inner voice
when she feels fear.

Good friends are a gift,
like sweet jelly beans.
They are never, ever
mean, mean, mean!

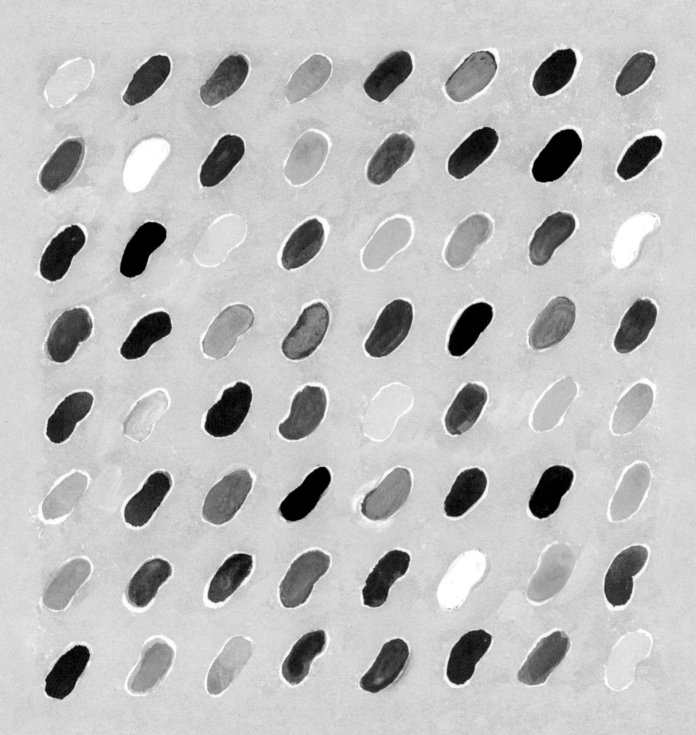